TALES OF THE LUCKY NICKEL SALOON,

SECOND AVE, LARAMIE, WYOMING, US OF A

Ken Rand

This one's for Mrs. Rachael Whitmore
(you can call her Rachael, or Mrs. Whitmore,
but I call her Mom),
who taught me how to laugh.

TABLE OF CONTENTS

Queen of the Dragons 7

The Problem with Mermaids 19

A Spider Poor Cowboy Rapt and Wide Lemon 31

The Grim Reaper Drops By 41

Charlie's in the Bottle 51

About The Author 59

About the Cover Artist 59

QUEEN O' THE DRAGONS

MICK was in love and not just a little. Every night after closing the Lucky Nickel Saloon, he took his profits and ambled three blocks down Laramie's Second Avenue and two doors around the corner to Dolly's Boarding House for Ladies and partook of the entertainments offered there by a certain Miss Emma Drummond, late of Saint Louie and points east.

"She's the prettiest girl in Wyoming," Mick reminded often, in case we regulars forgot, a little. He had a photo-graph taken of her. She looked like a lady in the picture, all gussied up in petticoats, a bustle, toting a parasol.

Us regulars, we daren't tell Mick what we thought. Even mud fence ugly, with a mustache better than Mick's, she looked as tolerable as any girl in Laramie in the entertainment trade. And Mick'd win no beauty contest himself unless he competed with mules. So, it didn't seem proper to opine unasked.

One day Mick came late to open and we regulars got close to calling the sheriff to see if he'd fallen down an outhouse somewhere, or got run over by a buggy, of which calamity he was more apt to suffer as he was hard of hearing. Us regulars, which meant me—I'm Tom Dooley, at your service—and Banky who fancies himself a gunfighter but ain't really, and Casper who has a glass eyeball and wears a patch over same and used to be an Indian fighter but is now a gambler but not a good one, and Charlie who drinks to excess, and Jack Thatcher who has a game leg and hadn't arrived yet—we all were mighty worried. But no, up he comes, finally, droopy-faced like somebody shot his favorite dog.

"What gives?" Casper asked in brotherly concern.

"Yeah, what?" Banky added.

"My life is over," Mick pronounced. We waited for him to drop the proverbial other boot as he set up for the day and he sighed a powerful lot of heavyweight sighs. But there was no egging him on. He worked at his own steady pace.

At last, he informed us. It seemed as how he'd asked the light of his life for to marry him and she turned him down.

"But why?" Charlie inquired.

"Yeah, why?" Banky added.

Seemed as how Miss Emma wanted Mick to pay off her contract to Miss Dolly first.

"Well," Casper put in, "we could help you. Pass the hat, so to speak. How much does your lady owe?"

"Yeah, how much?" Banky added.

Mick said and us who'd had breakfast near lost it.

"There's more," Mick noted, his countenance bleaker than any I'd seen outside a funeral home.

Given Mick's last news item, nobody wanted to hear, but he said anyway. "She wants me to give up the saloon trade and take up homesteading."

In the silence which ensued, you could have heard a cockroach fart.

We liked Mick right well enough, and if he took a fancy to a soiled dove, we figured more power to him. A man needs companionship. Besides, if he took a notion to marry such a one, that was okeydokey too, even if she demanded he become frugal in the process and do something noble like rescue her from some onerous contract. It might do Mick good to do something noble for a change. T'would keep him from going to hell for watering his whiskey.

But abandon the saloon business?

They'd build a cobblestone road twixt Laramie and Cheyenne afore us boys would cotton to such like. I saw my compatriots frown, shoulders hunched, brows furrowed, trying to figure how to talk Mick into accepting fate.

"The Lucky Nickel won't make you rich enough, I reckon," Charlie commiserated, "to buy out Miss Emma's contract, let alone give up the business. Too bad."

"Yeah, too bad," Banky added.

We all nodded agreement.

Besides, none of us could get credit anywheres else.

Mick just shrugged, saddened. He dusted off his picture of Miss Emma which he kept behind the bar to moon at.

Somehow we had to get him quit from thinking of Miss Emma, or the worst would happen. Mick was a clever enough businessman and no mistake, and if he set his mind to it, he'd figure a way to make his stake soon enough. I had to confer with the boys and see we got cleverer quicker.

I had no sooner thought up this thought when the day's first unregular customer sauntered in.

T'was a cowboy, judging by the chaps, dirty boots and spurs, and just in off the trail, judging by the smell.

He toted a fair-sized canvas bag in one hand. In the other, he dragged a rope with a leather loop on one end across the sawdust floor. He moseyed to the bar and ordered a beer.

"I'm seeking a buyer," he announces bold as a politician. He held up the loop connected to the rope on the floor.

"What's for sale?" I wondered.

"Yeah, what?" Banky added.

"Why, this here dragon," he responded, nodding at the loop he held up.

"Dragon?" Mick questioned, cupping his ear to hear better.

"Well, I don't see no dragon," Casper noted. He took out his glass eye, buffed it on his sleeve, put it back in, and shook his head.

"Me neither," Charlie joined in.

"Of course you don't," the cowboy agreed. He snorted and spat spitoonward. *Ping.* "It's an invisible dragon."

I'd never seen a dragon before, let alone an invisible one. And I'd traveled some, too.

We all sat or stood jaw-dropped, gazing at the place the fellow said his dragon sat.

"It don't bite none," the cowboy assured us in a whiny voice. He leaned away from the bar and reached over, rubbing a hand through the air just in front of the belt-like leather loop I now recognized as a collar, but one which could have hung loose on a Clydesdale's neck.

The cowboy held the collar up so a guy couldn't tell if he just held up the collar or if there was indeed an invisible neck through it, a body on one side sprawled on the floor and a head on the other side. The rope affixed to the collar drooped down to coil on the floor next to the cowboy's boots. He'd put the tote bag on the floor next to the leash.

The cowboy spat again. *Ping.* He was a good shot.

"I don't trade in livestock," Mick declared. He'd been polishing the same shot glass since the cowboy, who said his name was Slim, proposed to sell the dragon. "I prefer money."

"Reckon you do," Slim drawled, unperturbed. He puffed up whisker-specked cheeks preparatory to another shot at the spittoon fifteen feet away. *Ping.*

He gnawed off a thumb-sized bite of plug in yellow teeth and commenced to vigorous chewing again. We waited for him to speak. Me standing next to him, Mick behind the bar, Charlie over by the piano, Casper and Banky playing cards at their usual table, we all waited, polite-like. It was mid-morning and Jack Thatcher hadn't limped in yet.

"But this here dragon," Slim imparted, "ain't no regular dragon. No sir. I got her down to Utah, a place called Goblin Valley. S'posed to be haunted, I hear tell. Nobody goes in there but Indians, Mormons and other crazy folk, so the dragons what live there, they prosper." He leaned over the bar to Mick and added in a stage whisper, so we all could hear, "This here dragon is the Queen o' the Dragons."

"Do tell," I stated. As Slim was a few sheets to the wind and still upright, I took him for neither Indian nor Mormon, but what remained made his story somewhat plausible. Just a little.

"We had us some royalty in the Lucky Nickel once," Charlie observed. "Some Russian duke or other. Or was he Polish? Or was that some other saloon?"

Now, Mick, he was a right smart businessman as I said and I figured his poker face for a prelude to a boot in Slim's fanny, on account of if I saw the cowpoke's flim-flammery then surely Mick did too. Mick could tell from a snake oil peddler when he saw one, and I knew from embarrassing personal experience he could spot a marked deck across a smoky room.

But no. To my surprise, Mick looked halfway interested. "Queen o' the Dragons, you say?" he asked Slim.

"Yessir." Slim focused his sales pitch toward Mick, speaking up as he cottoned that Mick was near deef.

I have to admit it got me powerful puzzled watching Mick polish that damn shot glass so hard the rag frazzled.

"Well, what can you do with a dragon?" Casper inquired. He blinked his one good eye, stood from the table at which he'd sat, and inched closer to the critter. I expect Casper'd want to pet it, invisible or no, animal lover he is, but for fear he'd lose a hand. A one-eyed gambler is handicapped enough.

Slim laughed and tobacco juice sprayed. "What can you do with a dragon?" he repeated. For a moment, in which Banky unbuttoned his coat so he could grip his Colt if the need arose to shoot varmint, we thought Slim had insulted Casper, who wasn't bright but a good friend.

But no. Slim commenced into a windy narrative of dragon-owning benefits. Dragons, he informed us, made cracker guard animals, as they didn't cotton to rustlers nor coyotes. They made better beasts of burden than mules as they weren't as stubborn nor noisy and didn't kick. Like goats, they ate what you gave them, and not much at that, and they could go days without water like camels if the need arose for them to cross desert. They weren't as skittish as some horses when it came to fording rivers or suchlike. They had a way with sheep that made most dogs look lazy. They calmed nervous cows in storms better than an army of singing drovers.

"And they don't smell," he concluded, by which time Banky had joined Casper a few feet away from the critter in question. Charlie had come over too.

"See?" Slim stood over the dragon and inhaled. Charlie, Casper, and Banky did the same.

As Mick continued to look intrigued, I guess I was too. And if Mick had gone tetched in the head, so be it. I'd play along. He was a good barkeep and friend and I'll be the last fool to tell him he'd gone plumb loco. I hadn't told him so when he first declared his love for Miss Emma Drummond and I wasn't about to start now.

And Banky was a tad more temperamental with that Colt than my nerves could tolerate, which helped convince me to join in. He and Casper were tight, which didn't bode well for anyone who crossed Casper. So I stuck my nose over the collar, inhaled a draught and reported I couldn't smell the dragon either.

"Can't see it, neither," Charlie mumbled.

"Yet another advantage," Slim exclaimed. "Imagine sneaking a dragon into a boarding house or a train. Wouldn't rile the dragon none, but folks in the vicinity would raise cane. Futhermore, folks can steal horses, but what fool'd try to steal a dragon they can't see?"

It appeared to me as if Mick slipped yet another notch toward being full bore hoodwinked by Slim's flim-flammery. In my effort to avoid offense to him and my compatriots, I'd gone along with the sham too far to counter developments now with a dose of reality. So I stayed shut up. I reckoned it wouldn't hurt Mick a heap if he owned an invisible dragon. Sure he'd be out maybe a few bucks or a few drinks, but I'd seen him overcharge the occasional greenhorn or Chinaman and the drinks were watered down anyway so it all evened out.

Besides, it'd serve to distract him from Emma.

Slim also pointed out the dragon didn't bark and was house broken, as evidenced by its silence and lack of dragon shit.

By the time Slim talked Mick into paying five dollars and free drinks for the dragon if he threw in the collar, leash, and tote bag, I was in too far to buck, and mighty chagrined about it. I resolved to lose a few dollars to Mick in our next poker game to make up for my complicity.

In the tote bag, Slim uttered, lay rags for polishing the dragon and other useful equipage for the care of one's dragon.

We looked inside the bag and found what I took to be the usual old clothing items, bits of hardware, used utensils, saddle soap, and such stuff as one might expect among a cowboy's possibles. I stayed shut up, even when the boys in the bar nodded acceptingly as Slim pointed out how the bent metal fork he'd taken from the bag could be used for dragon grooming. He even demonstrated. He got down on the floor and extracted a splinter from the dragon's foot.

"Well, I don't see no splinter," Casper muttered, blinking.

"Ordinary splinters don't bode diddly to invisible dragons," Slim countered. "Invisible splinters give 'em fits."

By and by, Slim took his leave. He stood at the door, smiled us a so-long smile, and spat.

Ping.

"Where ought you to put the beast?" Charlie wondered.

"Yeah, where?" Banky added.

"Leave it to me," Mick declared as he sauntered around the bar and took the dragon in leash by one hand and the tote bag in the other and went into the back room, his quarters. "Mr. Bancroft," he communicated as he left, "please be so kind as to tend while I'm away."

Banky nodded, went around the bar, put on an apron, and affixed on his face a poor imitation of the stony frown for which Mick had acquired considerable notoriety.

We heard shuffling, tapping, and thumping from the back room and occasional cursing in Mick's voice. We heard nothing from the dragon.

Just then, Jack Thatcher limped in.

"Afternoon, boys," he waved his cane, plopped into his usual chair close by the bar and stretched out his game leg. He gave a puzzled look at Banky when the latter brought a pitcher. Jack inquired as to Mick's whereabouts.

"In the back tending to some business," Banky responded.

Jack took a pull at his beer, wiped the froth off his mustache, and coughed. "I reckon you-all've had yourself a mighty frisky time today."

"Well, what makes you say so?" Casper inquired.

"Yeah, what?" Banky added.

"I saw that cowboy fellow leaving the Lucky Nickel. He was laughing fit to bust a gut. Are you-all going to let me in on the joke or what have you?"

I looked at my companion's faces and realized they too had seen through the scam the cowboy named Slim had played on our friend Mick. And as I had done, they too had played along to avoid embarrassing Mick.

It took a few minutes to extract the information that they too went along with it because they each figured everyone else had bought into the scam and they didn't want to hurt anybody's feelings by pointing out how foolish they were. Why, they even thought I'd been hornswoggled too, a little.

"Fact is," Jack pointed out over his mug rim, "you all figured you each one was the onliest one not taken in." He laughed. "Now I see why that poke was laughing so hard. He humbugged you all."

When no one joined his jollity, he sobered up right quick. "What?" he inquired.

I nodded my head toward the back where we could still hear Mick fussing with his dragon.

"We wasn't took," Charlie declared, voice lowish, as if Mick might hear. "But Mick, he's out five bucks."

"And a couple drinks," Banky observed.

"It gets worse," I realized, as the notion occurred to me.

"Well, how so, Tom?" Casper demanded.

"Yeah, how?" Banky added.

"That cowpoke'll go to every bar in Laramie and brag up as how he pulled the wool over Mick's eyes. Mick'll be the laughing stock of the West."

"It ain't right," Jack insisted. "Not atall."

"There's more, Jack," I continued. I told him how Mick had proposed to Emma Drummond and how she'd turned him down, conditional-like, saying she wanted him to buy out her contract first, then quit the saloon business and homestead.

"Ever since he got amored of his lady friend," Jack declared, "Mick acts like somebody shot his lead duck."

"It just got as worst as it can get," Charlie added. "I calculate Mick'll be out of business by sundown and his lady love will give him the boot soon thereafter."

We all agreed. Banky began fingering his Colt as if fixing to drill him a cowboy or a whore and couldn't decide which. But he wore

Mick's apron and tended Mick's bar, which occasional duty he took serious, so no gunplay seemed in our immediate future, lucky for Slim or Emma.

"This morn, I worried we'd lose Mick to wedding bells," I recalled, "and see the end of the Lucky Nickel to boot. But now it looks like we'll see the end of the Lucky Nickel and ol' Mick won't win his true love's heart neither in the process."

"I'd druther lose the Lucky Nickel," Charlie maintained, wiping away a tear, "than lose my friend to a broken heart."

We all agreed, or at least said we did, but no solution to our new dilemma seemed imminent.

"What'll we tell Mick?" Charlie wondered.

"If anything," Banky put in.

"Well, we got to tell him something," Casper declared.

"Yeah," Jack decided. "T'wouldn't be right not to."

We heard the door to the back open and Mick reentered the bar. He appeared to be toting firewood or suchlike.

"I'll do what's right," I informed my friends, stiffening myself to the disagreeable task. They looked relieved I had volunteered. I didn't blame them diddly.

As I approached Mick, he handed me the contents of his arms. "Careful," he warned. "Paint's still wet."

He'd painted up some signs.

"What in tarnation?" I exclaimed.

"I recognized that fellow just in here," Mick announced as he escorted his dragon over by the piano.

"You did?" Banky asked.

"Yep. Howdy, Jack."

"Howdy, Mick."

The piano sat on a kind of raised platform, sort of stagelike. It wasn't like I'd seen at real show houses, but it kept the occasional drunk from tripping over the piano player, when Mick could afford one in his employ.

"You recognized him?" I persisted.

"Yep."

He tied up the dragon's leash to the piano and plopped the collar on the piano bench.

"Well, do tell," Casper insisted.

Mick put a rope thing around the piano stage area, a sort of courtesy barrier, like I'd seen at shows when they want to keep folk in lines or see they don't jump out at dignitaries or celebs. As I recall, Mick won it from a banker in a poker game or somesuch.

Anyway, it looked velvety and classy.

Maybe Mick heard Casper, maybe not. "Please hand me the second sign there," he requested of me. I put the signs down on the bar, next to where Mick had put the tote bag with the dragon maintenance stuff in it.

"Yep," Mick continued. "I recognized the sidewinder. Fellow name of Slim Yonkers, out of the Lazy Bar J up toward Tie Siding way. Sneaks into town of an occasional Saturday night and stops by Miss Dolly's, as is a cowboy's wont to do. Now, I'm not opposed to a hand taking his recreation as he sees fit, but this one, well—"

"Well, what?" Banky demanded. He took off Mick's apron, handed it to Mick, and stepped away from behind the bar.

Mick tied his apron on over his paunch and continued. "This fellow has taken a shine to my Emma. More than a regular fellow ought. More than just a little." You could see murder in Mick's usually unreadable eye and Banky's gun hand twitched in sympathy.

"You want me to speak to him?" Banky offered.

"I got me plan," Mick declared. "Gather round."

We did and Mick explained his plan.

It added up to this: if we went along, he'd insist Emma let him keep the bar open. We dithered a tad at first, but then he offered to tear up our bar tabs.

We joined his army. What are friends for?

DRAGON'S *Eggs*, the signs all over the bar read, *.50 cents ea. cooked as you like 'em.*

Hear the Queen o' the Dragons Play, the sign at the roped off area around the piano read. *Donations Gladly Accepted. Do Not Touch.*

We'd spread the word around town quick enough. The bar had filled up no later than lunch and had stayed so into the dinner hour and on. Banky had abandoned his table to help Mick behind the bar and business appeared brisk and steady.

A dandy, just off the train, sidled up to me at the bar and peered at my plate, a wondering look on his face.

"S'cuse me," he drawled from under a white mustache and around an odorous five-cent cigar, his white eyebrows like thatch over his eyes. He wore a white suit, like a Southern gent. "I'd be obliged if you could tell me what's going on here."

I put down my fork, finished chewing, wiped my lips with the napkin tucked neath my chin, and regarded him. "Why so?"

"I'm a journalist," he confessed, hooking thumbs in his vest. "Looks like an interesting story. I wondered if you'd share it with me."

I pondered the dude's inquiry a moment as he introduced himself as Sam Something, on his way by train to San Francisco, just stopped by to wet his whistle and soak up some local color.

I told him the story and recommended he find Slim Yonkers from the Lazy Bar J to confirm it, as he was the one who found the Queen o' the Dragons in the first place. I felt sure if the reporter interviewed Slim, the cowboy'd give credibility to the tale, as Slim'd be lynched if he asserted contrary words, thus irritating the good folks enjoying Mick's hospitality.

Sam interrupted my talk and dismissed himself to visit the privy out back. When he returned, he fidgeted a bit, scratching himself—"I got me this embarrassing and inconvenient, not to say burning, urinary tract problem," he confessed—then he asked about the silent piano music, where the donation tin filled steadily. I pointed out as how invisible dragons made invisible music, which fact is known even by Indians, Mormons, and other crazy people. He wrote it all down in a little notebook.

He bought me more invisible dragon eggs, scrambled as I like them, as we'd agreed he'd do in exchange for my story.

"How d'you know if they're undercooked?" he wondered.

Mick didn't hear, of course, nor did Banky or I would have feared for the reporter's life. "Mick's reputation as a cook is as great as his reputation as a bartender," I pontificated.

The reporter fellow nodded, satisfied at my sincerity, wrote down my words, checked his pocket watch, and searched for other folk to interview in the crowded room, went off to pee once or twice more. Then he left an hour or so later for the depot.

Miss Emma Drummond showed up close on to sundown, as she'd heard about the doings over to the Lucky Nickel. I watched she and Mick confer in whispers at the end of the bar. I couldn't hear, nor could the other regulars. But we all watched the exchange as best we could.

Miss Emma seemed a might perturbed at first. I reckoned by her expression that though she was delighted with Mick's apparent business success, she stuck by her guns on both the buying of her contract and the quitting of the saloon business in exchange for her hand.

Mick snuck her a quick gander at the roll of greenbacks he'd stashed in the moneybelt he always wore around his ample girth and her eyes sparkled. I knew of an instant Mick had won the day and he'd gotten her to let him keep the bar. She smiled and sat demurely at a table two gentlemen had vacated for her benefit.

As she waited for the invisible dragon eggs she'd ordered, she tapped a dainty foot in time to the invisible piano music played by the invisible Queen o' the Dragons.

Everybody in the place was either fooled, seemed like, or drunk, or maybe they were all going along, pretending, just a little. But it wasn't until near closing when Mick sauntered over to the piano and whispered something to the invisible dragon that I began to wonder.

Just a little.

THE PROBLEM WITH MERMAIDS

THE world is a strange place, except for the Lucky Nickel Saloon, where nothing much ever happens. Which is lucky, all in all, as us regulars like it tranquil.

Take Dan Murphy, for instance. A body expects Dan to ride in to Laramie now and then and pass the time of day telling whoppers. We always listened proper, for he told the best fish stories in these parts.

But when he let on he'd caught a mermaid on the Platte, we gave him what for. The result, I declare, was *not* tranquil.

Dan didn't appear at the time in a tale-telling mood, but we cranked it from him. Looking back, I reckon he just dropped by to wash down some dust—he looked a bit road-weary—but we got to egging him on and he let spill. Telling tales was such a habit, it was hard for him not to. I could see he wanted to swallow the words back right off, but too late. First he allowed as how he'd been fishing, then "I got me this mermaid," he uttered, then looked like he said something he hadn't ought.

"Well, what kind of bait did you use?" Casper inquired, eyebrow wiggling above his eye patch. "Worms, or did you offer to take her dancing?"

We all bust a gut laughing, except for Mick, who was deef and didn't catch all of what got said, and Jack Thatcher who hadn't arrived yet, and that newspaper fellow, Sam Something, who'd stopped to wet his whistle while waiting for a train to go back east. He'd dropped in a time or two as he traveled a lot and fancied our dive more than others and had become a semi-regular, you might say. Came in, asked a lot of silly questions, took notes in his little—bitty notebook, that sort of thing.

Now, we could poke fun at Dan, we knew, being friends, even though at first glance you'd figure Dan for an ornery cuss, as he sported a perpetual glower on his dark, bearded face like he'd et something disagreeable or Mexican. He had one black eyebrow above beady black eyes. That and the fact that he and an ox could play teeter-totter made him a force to be reckoned with.

We took Dan lightly on this particular tale, which we soon found we ought not. Dan did not favor us with so much as a grin. No, he just scrunched over the bar, shoulders arched like a steel bridge, and glowered into his mug. Mick also didn't laugh as nobody had told him what was up—he could lip read some—and he never laughed at paying customers before they'd paid.

"Well, I knew a girl once who ate worms," Casper offered from over by the piano where he worried a gin bottle. "Boy howdy, could she kiss. But her breath left much to be desired." His attempt to lighten up the situation fell like a dead pigeon.

I explained to Mick and he lip-read me and he chuckled but only a little. We intended our laughter to be good-natured, but Dan didn't see it. He took a lungful of a sigh, downed his brew in one gulp, wiped the foam off his formidable black mustache, slammed the mug down and stalked out, toward his wagon, hitched out front. He looked neither left nor right as he did so and he looked none too happy.

"Hey, Dan, old friend," Banky expressed in alarm as he followed the man to the batwing front doors, "what gives?" Dan had that red-eyed frowny glare which might indicate imminent gunplay on a lesser man.

"You figure Dan'll come back guns a-blazing, Tom?" Banky inquired of me.

Banky was a tolerable crack shot with his Colt which he always carried, and as Dan couldn't shoot worth diddly, it wasn't his life for which Banky feared when Dan stalked out. No sir. But Dan had had a snootful and when he did such, he was apt to strap on his rusty piece and ventilate the local woodwork. Dan couldn't shoot, but that wouldn't stop him from trying if he'd been righteous annoyed.

"Well, uh-oh," Casper observed. "Should we hightail it out of here and hide until the fireworks is over?"

Mick slapped down the mug he'd just pulled for Sam in front of the man with a solid smack and gave Casper a sternful eye, as he'd heard clear enough. Our taciturn Irish host wouldn't close for man nor Indian, no matter how riled either was.

"Should we go after Dan and try to humor him?" I wondered.

Banky spat spitoonward. *Ping.* "I reckon he's had time to repent, or arm himself, if he be so inclined." He unbuttoned his vest to facilitate more ready access to his Colt. The gesture was reflex, no doubt. As he and Dan were as tight as two mice in the same cuspidor, he wouldn't kill Dan for firing first, but he'd no doubt fire a few rounds to scare Dan back into sober contemplation of more agreeable options.

"Maybe he won't come back," Mick suggested. "His tab is pretty steep."

"You don't suppose he's planning to pay you with pickles." Banky stood near the batwing doors peering into the street. "Or with crackers." He spoke without turning.

We sat or stood at no good vantage to see what Banky saw as the Lucky Nickel was bereft of windows.

"Well, what?" Casper declared as he sauntered over to peer over Banky's shoulder. I joined them as did Sam.

Mick stayed at the bar. "What?" he added.

Dan had pulled a canvas tarp off his cargo on his wagon. Roped upright on the wagon bed sat a wooden barrel, a big one.

I saw water splash over the barrel rim and I suspicioned its contents.

Sam Something ran knobby fingers through bushy white hair, nodded toward the wagon and commented, "Boys, that ain't pickles nor crackers. It's a fish barrel."

I thought Dan might ask that we step outside to see the evidence of his fish story, but no. We got back away from the door so as not to impede him as he unloaded the cargo. Us boys, being polite, and so as not to affront Dan's pride, refrained from offering to help lift the barrel off the wagon and tote it up the steps into the saloon.

Which he did with much splashing, facial contortions, admirable grunts and such English language usage as would awe a muleskinner. When he finished, Dan wiped his brow on his sleeve and sighed as if he'd just suffered the annoyance of some mild but necessary exertion.

He stood beside the barrel, knobby fists anchored on hips, around which I noted with relief, nary gun belt, nor gun, and glared at us, one by one.

"Y'all took me for a liar, din't y'all? Well, I won't tolerate it. Which of you gents will be the first to step up and see for hisownself?"

We each took a gander into the barrel. When I took my turn, I confess I didn't know what to expect. I didn't expect to see a yellow-haired girl, maybe fifteen, sixteen or so, quite nekkid, sitting under water in the bottom of the barrel. We don't see many females in the Lucky Nickel, except for infrequent visits by Mick's fiancée, Miss Emma Drummond. I'd never seen a white girl out West over eight years old shirtless, except whores, let alone under water in a barrel in the Lucky Nickel.

I might have been tempted to stare at her chest above her crossed arms, as she seemed unabashed to be uncovered. But her scowly demeanor tempered all lusty thought. She wouldn't meet my eye and she looked as sulky as a housewife with muddy bootprints on her parlor rug.

Meanwhile, Dan glared at me as if to say without saying that he disapproved of me looking at what he'd invited me to look at. I guess the glare come of his upset that we'd called him a liar, as our laughter implied. I felt mighty chagrined.

And you'd figure any normal person sitting under water in the bottom of a barrel might elect to sit cross-legged in the confined space, if they chose to sit at all. But no. The female in the barrel sat with her tail curled around her hips.

From the waist down she was fish, and it wasn't until I noticed her tail aflutter in the water, the way an impatient young lady might flutter a fan in agitation waiting on a late-arriving gentleman caller, that I noticed a fishy odor.

After we'd all had our look, we stood away from the barrel to give the lady a little privacy. We didn't want to be so ungentlemanlike as to stare, especially under Dan's glower.

"Well, she's a mermaid for certain sure," Casper pontificated, quiet and breathless. The eyebrow above his eye patch wiggled snakelike.

"I warrant we owe you an apology, Dan." Banky rebuttoned his vest over the Colt and extended his hand to Dan in contrition. Dan took it and shook it, ever the gentleman. We all took turns offering handshakes in apology, then nursing the appendage thus wounded in Dan's iron grip.

"I see a problem," Sam Something observed, thumbs anchored in his white vest.

"What?" Banky wondered. Spit. *Ping.*

"Yeah, what?" Dan added.

"Have you had occasion to speak to your, er, catch?"

"What do you mean?" Dan asked.

"When you caught her, did she say anything? Tell you to go about your business and leave her be? Anything like that?"

"I recall being a touch distracted at the time." Dan took off his hat and scratched at his thick hair, a patch of prairie grass after a big blow. He seemed reluctant to go on.

"What did she say?" Sam persisted.

"I think, Mister Reporter, sir, that words between a fisherman and his catch ought to be free from public scrutiny."

"He means he ain't going to say," Banky interpreted.

"But you reeled her in anyway, didn't you?" Sam pressed.

Dan stared at the floor, mumbled and shuffled foot to foot as if he had to pee. We feared for Sam's safety for a spell, but Dan didn't throttle the nosy little man. In time, Sam pried from Dan a truth any man'd be reluctant to reveal to even his best drinking buddies.

Dan Murphy had used a net. He'd *netted* the mermaid.

His shame was palpable. Dan was the best fisherman among us, despite tales tall enough as to impress Jonah, and we were all tolerable good even with a stick pole, some twine, and a bent pin. We couldn't meet his eye for a long time, but I resolved to make up with him as he owed me two dollars.

"Why was the lady in the Platte, after all?" Sam wondered.

"Yeah, why?" Banky joined in.

Dan glared, arms crossed and lips shut.

"We know the mermaid is not native to these parts, am I correct, gentlemen?" Sam continued.

"I've never heard to the contrary," I assured him.

"Gentlemen, I've traveled the world. I'm familiar with the customs of a hundred foreign countries. I have encountered tales about mermaids in twenty foreign climes. And as I am fluent in a dozen languages, I feel if we can persuade our guest to surface, perhaps we can solve the problem."

"Well, how do we get her to come up?" Casper pondered.

"Oh, all right." Dan looked as if he itched to toss his beer mug across the room or chew it, whichever. Instead, he gulped down its contents and walked back over to the barrel. "If y'all'll hush a bit, I'll fess up and solve your wondering."

Dan leaned over the barrel, took a breath, held it in puffy cheeks, and stuck his head under water, much of which splashed over the sides. Bubbles rose and a body might have thought Dan and the mermaid conversed as we heard odd sounds emerging with the bubbles. They sounded argumentative.

At last, Dan surfaced, drippy as a bird dog after a good hunt, and demanded, "Okay, y'all turn your backs now."

"What?" Banky inquired.

Dan bunched fists like two nine-pound hammers and gave us a glare as brooked no dispute. We turned our backs forthwith.

In a moment we heard more splashing, then what sounded like a woman—or a lady, but we couldn't tell as the words were muffled and indistinct whispered, nor was I sure if I heard any cussing in the utterances—and Dan's voice whispering, only it sounded more contrite than I'd ever heard from Dan, so I figure he was talking with the mermaid who, as far as I could tell, had risen from the barrel for what purpose Dan had yet to reveal. Still, I kept my back turned so as to comply with Dan's wish and to avoid embarrassment to the mermaid by staring at her chest as I'd done when she sat in the barrel sulking.

"Okay," Dan announced, "y'all can turn around now."

We did and saw Dan standing shirtless, sopping, and hairy-chested beside the barrel in which we could now see the mermaid wearing Dan's wet shirt as big as a tent on her. A body might have figured we looked upon a gal standing in a barrel if not for the fact we'd already seen she had a tail where other folks had legs.

The mermaid looked terrible put out, as well as sad and shy. She'd moved a gob of wet blonde hair off her forehead and although she looked downcast, we could see how pretty she was.

"Boys," Dan announced, "I'd like you to meet Miss Elizabeth Suzette Cockette."

We all nodded and howdied. Casper doffed his hat and Banky buffed his boots on his calfs. He didn't spit.

"Lizzy," Dan continued, addressing the mermaid, "these here are the boys."

"How-dee, zee boys," Lizzy the mermaid howdied in what sounded to me like a French accent. Or maybe Greek.

We did personal introductions during which we all bowed or nodded and said our say, all somewhat uncomfortable in the presence of a young girl-woman—I still hadn't figured out for sure yet which, except she was a mermaid—whose upper torso we'd just had a gander at.

"And now, for the problem," Sam interjected. He'd been the last to be formally introduced to the lady-woman-girl mermaid and he did so with the dignity one expects from a fellow who'd interviewed queens, Arabs and potentates in far lands and who'd traveled even more easter than Saint Lou.

"If you ain't the most nosy critter—" Dan began to fume. The mermaid lit into him in French or Greek or whatever, and Dan, to our surprise, listened. After a few seconds of high-velocity jabber, Dan's shoulders hunched, his head bowed and he began shuffling his toe in the sawdust. We got the message the mermaid was giving him a tongue-lashing that sounded powerful enough to melt the varnish off the bar.

He muttered in mermaid-talk, which surprised us all again, and nodded. He sighed and faced us.

"Now, boys," he informed us, "Lizzy ain't never been in a bar before, and she's a might put out."

"But that ain't your problem," Sam persisted.

Once again the mermaid intervened, preventing Dan from bashing the soda crackers out of Sam Something. To our amazement again, Dan answered in mermaid gibberish.

"What're they talking?" Banky asked, in general.

"French," Sam told us she spoke, as did Dan.

Just then a commotion in the street interrupted Dan as he was fixing to explain what the blue blazes was going on, including as how he knew how to speak French.

We crowded toward the batwing doors where we saw, coming at us, the sheriff and the strangest entourage I'd ever seen.

The folks with the sheriff looked as if they'd escaped from a circus. Among them stalked a tall man, must have been seven or eight foot, and a lady who made the term 'stout' seem an understatement, and a woman with a beard thicker than Dan's, and one person who looked both man and woman, and a slick, mustachioed fellow in tails and a top hat I took to be a circus ringmaster, and a three feet tall fellow toting a shotgun twice as long as he was tall.

None toted a rope, but they looked awful lynch-mob like.

"Now," Sam declared, hiding behind the bar, out of the line of fire, "*there*'s a problem."

With a glance at Lizzy's gloomy countenance, which matched Dan's, I finally figured what Sam'd figured.

Runaway lovers, Dan and his mermaid. And here come pa with the shotgun. Or somesuch. There was more to it, no doubt, but like as not, I was close.

"You're in a heap of trouble, Dan Murphy," Banky declared.

"Don't I know it," Dan answered, but he looked at Lizzy when he said it, not at the mob.

"Zere would no a problem be, mon cherry," Lizzy glared at Dan, hands on her hips, "eef to me you 'ad listened." In my minds eye, I visualized a rolling pin in her dainty fist.

"If you hadn't jumped in the crick—" but Dan's protest fell beneath the onslaught of the mob's entrance.

Everybody talked at once. The ringmaster demanded somewhat of Lizzy in stern fatherly French tones. The dwarf threatened Dan with his shotgun and a flea-sized squeaky voice. Dan ignored him as if he were a toddler wielding a slingshot. Several ladies in the entourage, including the person whose sex appeared in open dispute, descended on Lizzy like a pack of wild hens, yakking and fussing.

The sheriff tried to hush everybody and get them to talk one at a time. As usual, nobody paid him much attention.

Mick looked as happy as his otherwise taciturn features allowed to see such a crowd in the saloon so early in the day and no shots fired yet.

Folks came in off Second Ave wondering what gives.

Dan took it quiet, arms folded, glowering, as did Lizzy, a tiny imitation of Dan's glower on her wet, pretty face.

Sam observed the folderol from behind the bar, where I hunkered along with Banky, Mick, Sam, and Casper.

I'd seen a circus before, but never in the Lucky Nickel, as far as I can recall. 'Twas a sight and no mistake.

Sam whispered into Banky's ear. Banky frowned suspicious and put a hand over his Colt as if Sam had asked to borrow it or somesuch else improper.

After more whispers betwixt the two, which I strained to overhear but didn't, the light dawned on Banky, his eyebrows rose and he nodded agreement. Whereupon he spat—*ping*—withdrew the Colt, and fired a shot at the ceiling.

Nothing prompts attention as a shot fired in a room full of arguing people. Folks scattered like flushed quail. The hens flustered and fainted, as evidenced when some chairs by the fat lady thunderously collapsed. The sheriff drew a pistol and while looking around for someone to cuss at, dropped the piece and ducked as it discharged. The bullet tore the heel off the tall guys' boot and he fell from over *there* to over *here*. I wanted to yell "timber" as he fell but didn't.

I saw Mick's lips move, assessing the furniture damage as his hands protectively surrounded his exposed glassware.

In the ensuing silence, Sam Something, back-east reporter and world traveler, expert in mermaids, French, and who knows what all else, took a stance on a chair and waited for everybody to pay him attention. Which we did, by and by.

"It looks," Sam pontificated, "like we got a problem."

"Well, you keep saying that," Casper responded, annoyed.

"And I mean to solve it before my train arrives," Sam countered. He took out his pocket watch, flicked it open, gazed at it, clicked it shut, repocketed it. "One hour."

For a time everybody talked at once again, until Sam gave a nod to Banky, who fired another shot into the ceiling. Everybody shut up again and Sam continued.

He sounded more like a lawyer than a reporter as he proceeded to question the witnesses present and in jig time, figure out what the Sam Hill was going on.

It seems Dan had gone down to Grand Encampment a few months back to visit kin and while there, he took in a circus. He fell in love straight away with one of the attractions, one Miss Elizabeth Suzette Cockette, mermaid, which love she returned.

But the star-crossed lovers parted on account of Dan's commitment to a laborer job in Laramie and hers to the circus, which had a schedule to keep. They parted with heartfelt promises to meet again and, well, get together, so to speak. Exactly how that would be done wasn't specified in Sam's interrogation, but I do admit to my own curiosity.

Not a week past, Dan heard the circus was swinging back along the Union Pacific from Sacramento, through Salt Lake City, then through Laramie and points east. Sam himself had seen the show in question in Carson City and knew of the mermaid. His trip east paralleled the circus', more or less.

"Now comes the part where the two lovebirds decide to elope," Sam related. "Stop me if I get this wrong, son," he suggested to Dan. "You and Miss Cockette decide to elope at Medicine Bow on account of, Miss Cockette, your guardian, the ringmaster here, whose name I've forgotten—sorry, sir—would disapprove, as you well knew, on account of your age. Anyway, you set out and you start talking about marriage with Dan, and Dan says something like, 'What the goldurn hell you talking about? Marriage? Whatever for?' Like as though the subject had never come up before betwixt you, which maybe it hadn't. And at this point—correct me if I'm wrong, Miss Cockette—you take umbrage, get angered and jump out of the wagon and dip into the crick from whence Dan is obliged to fish you out. How'm I doing so far?"

"I didn't say 'goldurn hell,'" Dan protested. "Something near like it, but I don't swear in front of a lady. No sir."

"And even zoe 'is mine 'e changes," Lizzy observed, "marry heem weel I no."

"She says she ain't going to marry him," Banky interpreted.

"*Now*, we're at the real problem, ain't we?" Sam intoned.

Further interrogation, Sam officiating, ensued during which the dilemma became clear—Lizzy wanted to marry Dan, Dan was reluctant to get hitched, the ringmaster-guardian wanted what he called "justice done of his little girl, if required," and Mick wanted somebody to pay for the broken furniture.

At some point, Sam took out his pocket watch, frowned, and yelled above the hubbub. "Is there a preacher in the house?"

A body would've thought it unlikely there'd be a preacher in the Lucky Nickel, but it had been an odd day. The circus was in the saloon, so why not a preacher?

He stepped from the crowd of townsfolk attracted by gunshots and the to-do. Reverend Avery Morgan, he declared himself, and though I don't recall ever breaking bread or getting drunk with him, he seemed a right nice fellow, a devout man of God, and not a temperance fool, bless him.

"Your Reverendship," Sam proposed, "would you be averse to marrying Dan Murphy, citizen of Laramie, to Lizzy Cockette?"

The all-hell which broke loose at Sam's question ended abrupt as Banky added another hole in the ceiling. I foresaw the need for some carpentry atop the Lucky Nickel before the rainy season set in. Anyway, quiet followed.

Sam got down from the chair and had a whisper conference with the ringmaster, with Dan, with Lizzy and with the preacher. And with Mick.

Then Dan had a whisper talk with the ringmaster, with Lizzy, with the preacher, and with Mick.

Then Lizzy had a whisper chat with the ringmaster, with the preacher, with Dan, and with Mick.

Then—well, then, so on and so forth.

It came to pass we had a wedding in the Lucky Nickel Saloon. Dan Murphy got hitched to Miss Elizabeth Suzette Cockette and she became Mrs. etc. The women folk, circus and townie, bearded and clean-shaven, skinny and not, and even the semi-woman, all had theirselves a good cry. The menfolk drank a lot but didn't get in too many fights. Nobody got killed.

Sam disappeared in the fuss after the wedding to catch his train before I could ask how he managed to keep everybody happy meeting their various and contradictory needs.

The circus bunch left in a flurry of singing, gunfire and carousing the like of which Laramie hadn't seen since they hung Big Nose George. I discovered too late Dan Murphy had left with the circus along with his bride.

In fact, I found myself alone in the Lucky Nickel except for Mick who stood behind the bar, whistling an Irish ditty, as happy as a cowboy on Saturday night.

"What gives?" I asked.

He stopped whistling and looked at me like I'd just asked him how many boots he wore on each foot. He cupped his ear and said "What?"

"I mean," I clarified, a bit louder, "how come Dan went along with getting hitched? I thought he was averse to the notion. What swung him, so to speak?"

"Couple things. First, I forgave him his bar tab."

"You *what?*"

"He brought enough business in today to make up for it."

"Huh. But I never figured Dan to be the kind who'd run away with a circus."

"You figured wrong. Seems as how Sam knew the circus had lost their strongman in a bar fight back in Winnemucca. That reporter fellow suggested the circus hire Dan as their strongman. This pleased the ringmaster as he got to keep Lizzy on—he was fearsome she'd leave, you know—and he got his strongman in Dan."

"Huh. So Dan wanted to run away and join the circus?"

"Truth."

"That answers for Dan and the ringmaster and the other circus types, right enough. But what of Lizzy? I mean, she told as how even if ''is mind 'e changes, I marry 'im no.' Or somesuch."

Mick took in a powerful big sigh and leaned on the bar, wonderment on his otherwise stoic countenance. "You ain't going to believe this," he warned.

"I've seen a mermaid in a barrel in the Lucky Nickel, a naked one. I've seen me Dan Murphy talking to a mermaid in a barrel with his head underwater in the Lucky Nickel. I've seen me a circus right here in the—"

"You ain't going to believe—"

"—I've seen a wedding betwixt a mermaid and Dan Murphy—"

"Ain't going to."

"Huh." I shrugged. "If you say so."

"Remember the problem to which Sam Something kept referring?"

"Yep. I never heard what it was though. Did I?"

"He told me afore he left."

"What?"

"Mermaids are kin to fish."

Mick let me chew on that a spell, no doubt enjoying the consternation which unfolded on my face.

"Lordy," I gasped, awed. If I'd been chewing at the time, I'd swallowed my plug for certain sure. "Say it ain't so."

"It's so. Lizzy talked Dan into giving up fishing."

"Huh," I declared, flabbergasted.

"Truth. He was that much in love." Mick's tone reflected his awe. He shook his head, went about his business, cleaning glassware, whistling and suchlike.

And when, a few days later, a cowboy entered the Lucky Nickel Saloon hauling an invisible dragon on a leash, we threw both cowboy and dragon out into the street with nary a word, as we'd had our fill, thank you.

Yessir, the world is a strange place, except for the Lucky Nickel, where nothing much ever happens. Which is a lucky thing, all in all, as us regulars like it tranquil.

A SPIDER POOR COWBOY RAPT AND WIDE LEMON

NOT until the stranger hunching over the bar reached for his whisky and his hand passed through the glass did I figure out why he seemed so peculiar.

"Now, ain't that amazing?" I said to nobody in particular.

He looked mighty insubstantial. I could see the batwing doors through his scarecrow-thin torso, the hitching post beyond, and muddy Second Avenue beyond that. He looked to be no more than a suggestion of a man, something somebody thought up and then decided "nevermind" halfway through.

"Do you not see what I don't see?" asked Casper, whose one good eye watered. He took out his glass eyeball, buffed it on his sleeve and put it back in and blinked. It didn't help.

"Reckon I don't." Banky flicked his vest away from the handle of his ever-ready Colt, in case whatever strangeness was going on required gunplay. Mick the barkeep's lip twitched causing his formidable black mustache to tickle his nose and make him sneeze, but otherwise he remained his stony-faced self. Charlie lay passed out under a table by the piano and Jack Thatcher hadn't arrived yet.

Nobody else was in the bar—it was still early—except us regulars and the stranger who wasn't all there.

"Well," Casper intoned, "I guess now I've seen everything. Or not, if you take my meaning."

"Reckon I do," Banky responded. He bent at the waist, examining the so-far silent stranger's feet. Those feet did not touch the floor. At first glance, the toes of the ethereal appendages seemed to be anchored under the brass bar rail as if to keep their owner from floating away, off to Heaven or wherever. But no. Banky pointed out the toes didn't touch the bar rail underside—the stranger floated twixt floor and rail.

The stranger made another attempt to grab the whisky glass. His hand passed through it and he sighed. It sounded like a cold wind in a graveyard.

"Begging your pardon, sir." Mick cleared his throat. "I notice you're having a bit of trouble grasping your drink."

The stranger looked at Mick with sad see-through eyes and nodded his see-through head.

"You'll pardon me, sir," Mick continued, "if I remark that you seem a tad, uh, insubstantial, so to speak."

The stranger nodded again. His sigh was so cold I buttoned the top button of my coat.

"And," Mick continued in his methodical Irish way, "if I offered you a hand and, like, poured the drink down your throat, it'd probably go right through you like Texas chili and splash on the floor undrunk. Am I right so far?"

The stranger nodded again. I could see a tear in one eye.

"And how did you intend to pay for your drink?" Mick got to the point. "I mean, if substantial things like drink go right through you and you can't take hold of a whisky glass, I'll wager coin'd drop right through your pockets."

The stranger looked puzzled for a moment. He pulled his pockets inside out and as Mick predicted, they were empty.

It's downright embarrassing to see a grown man cry, whether he's all there or not.

Mick offered the stranger a bar towel to wipe his eyes, holding it out so the stranger could drip onto it. Banky turned away and busied himself refilling his lip with chaw so as not to see the stranger's wimpy display of emotion. Casper polished his eye again, I got a coughing fit, Charlie remained passed out, and Jack Thatcher hadn't arrived yet.

In due time (I reckon t'was in due time—I'm not conversant as to what constitutes "due time" for ghosts.) the stranger quit snuffling. Mick tossed the soggy towel aside and reached to pick up the stranger's whisky glass.

Banky, ever quick on the draw, intercepted same, downing the contents in a gulp. "Waste not, want not," he pontificated, wiping his lips with the back of his non-gun hand. He tossed a nickel on the bar.

"I'm sorry, bartender," the stranger spoke at last. He sounded hollow-like, as if he spoke from the bottom of a well, and mighty contrite to boot. "I've never been dead before and I, I—I'm sorry."

Mick's formidable shoulders lifted an inch, his taciturn way of accepting the apology.

"Well, stranger," Casper piped up, "how'd you happen to, uh, you know—"

The stranger peered at Casper with watery eyes and frowned, puzzled. Casper shuffled, head-bobbing, tongue-tied.

"Yeah," Banky intervened, "how'd you get kilt?"

The stranger uttered another graveyard sigh, parted his vest, and displayed the .45-caliber sized hole in his shirt, beyond which his heart no longer beat. Through the hole, I could see Charlie waking up.

"My name's Butch Parker," the stranger began, "late of Green River." His tale unfolded and we learned thus:

Butch foremanned at the Lazy Bar-K cattle ranch out west between Rock Springs and Reliance. He was on his way home after selling a herd back in Kansas City. But when he got off the train to stretch his legs in Laramie during a dinner stop the night afore, somebody jumped him to take his poke. He protested the robbery and his assailants did him in with one shot.

"I come to and stood over myself, realizing I'd been kilt. Saddened me good and proper." He nodded toward the now empty glass. "I needed that drink."

"So you chose to get drunk at the Lucky Nickel," I remarked. "Heard about us down the line, did you? Stories about invisible dragons and mermaids and circuses and such?"

"No. You was just closest."

"Well, tarnation," Casper gasped, good eye twitching. He ran out the back door into the alley. In a second, he ran back in. He walked up to the stranger and looked him right in the eye, blinking. "That's you out there, all right. Well, you—you're dead."

"Reckon I know that," Butch confirmed.

"So that *was* a shot I heard this morning," Mick recalled, "just as I opened up." He tapped his ear and shook his head. "I don't hear so good, sometimes."

Banky crouched, flint-eyed, gun hand ready. "Why those no good cussed yellow-bellied low-down dirty rotten sons of—"

"What do we do now?" I wondered.

"We're a tad late, helpwise," Mick observed.

Silence ensued.

At last, Butch piped up: "Mind if I stick around and, you know, sort of haunt your place?"

Mick's jaw dropped open and he stammered something that sounded like he was strangling on a lump of Miss Dolly's Boarding House for Ladies's almost-mashed potatoes. Casper's glass eye almost popped out, and Banky almost dropped his gun.

Charlie, who'd just resumed consciousness, appeared over my shoulder and peered bleary-eyed at Butch. He focused at last, and pointed. "Tom, it's a gho-gho—"

"A ghost," I finished. "His name is—"

But Charlie didn't stay for introductions. He ran, suspenders flapping, still clutching his empty gin bottle, into the street, screaming like he'd been scalped.

"Now, you understand, Butch," Mick explained, "why I'd druthern't have my saloon haunted. Charlie's my friend, and he pays his tab, now and then. I reckon he'll go drink someplace else now where there ain't no ghosts."

"I'm sorry," Butch squeaked. He sighed, as broken-hearted as a mamaless calf. "But I got no place else to go."

Just then, Jack Thatcher arrived. "Say," he said as he hobbled in, "I just saw Charlie running—" Then, eyes bugged out, he pointed at the ghost with his cane and commenced to jabber and drool. "A gho—gho—" and so on, before he took flight—foot, stump, and cane flying every whichaway, like a hog skittering on ice—for a more agreeable locale.

"And Jack Thatcher," Mick said, pointing, voice raised, "he's been steady custom since '88. That's two of my regulars—"

"I said I'm sorry," Butch insisted, "but I got no other place to go."

"You mean to say," Mick inquired, "you're going to stay here whether I like it or not?"

"Ghosts are supposed to haunt places, ain't they?"

"Well, yeah, but—"

"I told you, I got no other place—"

"Land O' Goshen." Mick threw up his hands. "I'm arguing with a dead man."

"Well, maybe we should go get the sheriff." Casper blinked. "And the coroner. We got us a dead body in the alley needs burying."

"Right," Banky said, quick as ever, striding to the door, "maybe if we bury Butch here, his spirit will go away." He gave the ghost a dirty look as he departed.

"I'm sorry—" Butch began.

"Oh, shut up," Mick finished. Mick sauntered over to the end of the bar, summoning me and Casper with a twitch of his burly head. We huddled out of Butch's earshot.

"Boys," Mick whispered, "I reckon I'm in a fix and no mistake. If this ghost insists on staying, I won't get no paying customers. I mean, you guys pay your tabs come payday, usually, and all, but..."

"Well, I guess I know what you mean, Mick, old friend." Casper frowned. "Ain't nobody but us regulars, I reckon, would stay put in a saloon frequented by a ghost. I mean, we know you. We wouldn't take our custom elsewhere, come hell or high water. But other folks—"

"You're in a heap of trouble, Mick." I shook my head. My payday wasn't due for two weeks yet and I'd already run up a two dollar tab. No, the Lucky Nickel didn't earn its keep, meager as it was, from us regulars—me and Casper, Charlie, Banky, and Jack Thatcher. It depended on the custom of passing-through cowboys and miners, the odd townie, and business folk that traveled by train or hung around the station a block and a half west of the saloon, like that reporter fellow, Sam Something, who dropped by now and then and wrote stories about us. They sure as shooting wouldn't cotton to a ghost at their elbow, weeping in his beer.

And it wasn't as if Mick didn't like ghosts. His liberal reputation earned praise from San Francisco to Chicago. He served Indians, Chinamen, and the occasional Mormon just like he would any whiteman, watering down their liquor not much at all.

"Well, we can't throw him out," Casper pondered. "He's too insubstantial to grab a holt of."

"We sure can't scare him off," I added. "*He*'s the ghost."

"Maybe burying him'll do the trick," Mick muttered. We all went about our business, Mick figuring his losses, Casper polishing his eye, me drinking the day by. And Butch, weeping ghostly at the bar.

WE passed the hat and coughed up fifty cents each for a nice pine box to put Butch's body in. We got our old friend Preacher Avery Morgan drunk enough to officiate at the burying in the pauper's field on the other side of the tracks, but burying Butch Parker didn't answer.

Butch attended his own funeral and cried and carried on such that the preacher ran off scared—we hadn't gotten him drunk enough. Me, Mick, and Casper finished the praying as best we could, being inexperienced in the practice.

Then we did the shoveling.

And Butch, right after the burying, went on back to the Lucky Nickel, took his place at the bar, staring sadly at the empty shot glass Mick put before him as sort of a monument to mark his spot—as if somebody would want to take that stool—and resumed his graveyard moaning and weeping.

Banky glowered at him. "I thought burying you would make you go away."

Butch shrugged and wept.

Come the third day of practically no business in the Lucky Nickel, except us regulars—free drinks persuaded Charlie and Jack Thatcher to resume their custom—when that reporter, Sam Something, walked in.

"I heard about your ghost away back in Saint Lou," he said, puffing on a cigar clenched between his teeth. He anchored thumbs in a white vest and bobbed his white eyebrows.

"What of it?" Mick snarled. His usual placid demeanor had begun to crack under the pressure of his pending poverty.

"I'd like to interview the fellow," the reporter said.

Butch almost stopped crying for a moment as he overheard.

Mick shrugged. "Suit yourself."

And Sam Something did. He sauntered over and took the stool next to Butch and commenced to interview the spook. We couldn't hear what they said as Sam spoke low and Butch replied in kind. Now and then, the two would turn to look at us most peculiar-like, as if examining a herd of two-headed lambs. Now and then, Butch would take to weeping and moaning plenty loud and Sam would try to pat him on the back only to jerk away amazed as his hand passed through the skinny ghost's back. Then Sam'd shake his head in wonder and continue talking to Butch, taking notes in his little-bitty notebook.

Soon, the reporter stood. He extended his hand as if to shake with the ghost, momentarily forgetting Butch's insubstantiality. Butch broke down in another boo-hooing fit, Sam shook his head, and came back to sit with us live types on the other side of the room—we gave Butch a wide birth, leaving him alone in his misery.

"Boys," Sam said, "that's the saddest ghost I ever seen." He tugged at his shaggy white mustache and relit his cigar.

"Well, how many sad ghosts have you seen?" Casper asked.

Sam ignored Casper. "And I know what to do about it."

"You do?" Mick all but sat in Sam's lap, so evident was his interest. We all paid attention as the reporter explained.

"Turns out Mr. Parker ain't Christian, y'see. No sir. He's Hindoo."

"Well, he don't look Hindooish," Casper observed.

"And he requires a proper Hindoo burial to lay his soul to rest. I've seen the ritual in my extensive foreign travels and I believe I know how to do the honors."

IT took some doing to get Butch Parker's body dug up so we could rebury it proper and Hindoolike. It wasn't because anybody cared one way or the other (he was, after all, in the pauper's graveyard). In fact, Preacher Morgan was glad to pitch in once we got him good and drunk, to which condition he was not averse to when we told him what we had in mind.

We couldn't find the body.

It had rained like a cow pissing on a flat rock the night Sam told us what needed doing and he agreed to stay over a few days to help us in the doing thereof. The rain had washed away the grave markers and fresh dirt and we couldn't figure under which mud hole slept Butch's body, whose ghost took the dismal development as tearfully as we'd come to expect.

After we dug up and re-buried three suspects (us regulars dug and Sam supervised on account of he had a bad back) we finally come across the right cadaver.

Then we performed us a genuine Hindoo burial ceremony.

Except for Sam who complained of a skin condition, we all had to wear dresses for the ceremony. Kilts, Sam called them, and he said the burying priests in Hindoostan all wore them. We got some help from Miss Dolly, who ran Miss Dolly's Boarding House for Ladies three blocks down Second Ave and around the corner two doors down, and where Miss Emma Drummond, Mick's fiancée, worked in the entertainment trade, and her fellow entertaining ladies also labored.

The required sandals were make-do throw-away hide clumps from Joe Meecham's Tannery tied on with twine. We wondered how the Hindoos managed to ride a horse wearing dresses and sandals, but we didn't say diddly. If it meant getting shut of our haunt, we'd go along.

But it was a trial and no mistake.

I'd worn facepaint once when I got drunk at an Arapaho hunting camp, but I don't recall ever being drunk enough to wear flowers in my hair.

I figure the dance step Sam taught us might come in handy some day when I had to scare the hell out of a griz bear, but I was too stewed to remember all the words to the song he taught.

Just bits and pieces:

"As I wig doubt inner stretch of tomatoes,
A sigh weak downer tomato and hay,
A spider poor cowboy rapt and wide lemon,

A ripped and wide leanin' ass goldfish decay."

Or somesuch.

All us regulars took part as substitute Hindoo priests, as Sam insisted was needed to properly lay Butch to rest.

The ceremony, held on a bitty hill within rock-throwing distance of the Lucky Nickel, began at high noon of a Saturday, and attracted quite a crowd. We were so intent on doing the ceremony right we paid no nevermind to the snickers and guffaws from the gawkers.

And right as the last shovelful of dirt fell on the Hindoo grave of the late Mr. Butch Parker, his shade vanished in a silent puff of not-there-anymore-ness.

Which event Mick greeted with a nod, Banky touched off a few rounds in the air, Casper whooped and his glass eye popped, Charlie regained consciousness, and Jack Thatcher took off his wooden leg and did a one-legged backward somersault.

We all got out of our Hindoo costumes and got into our regular duds and went to the Lucky Nickel to get drunk. Mick did a brisk business, what with all the gawkers and on-lookers who'd tagged along to help celebrate.

At the bar, I sidled up to Sam Something. "You know, I felt right silly wearing that stuff you said we had to wear."

"Do tell."

"And that dancing and carrying on you said was required."

"Indeed."

"And the warpaint and suchlike."

"What about 'em?"

"Tell me true," I leaned in, whispering so nobody else could hear, "did we really have to do all that stuff to get rid of Butch's ghost?"

Sam's thatchy white eyebrows rose into his thatchy white hair and he uttered a snort that, at first, I took for derision. "Whisky for this man," he called to Mick, "as much as he'll take afore passing out."

"Mighty kind of you, Sam, uh—"

"You are a right smart gent, I declare." Sam patted me on the back. "The reward is justified. As is the truth for which you've asked. And here 'tis.

"Your ghost weren't Hindoo atall. I made up all that."

I had "You what?" in my throat ready to come out when I realized maybe I didn't want anybody else to hear what Sam had to say. So I just nodded for him to go on, as he did, thankfully not too loud.

"I made it up because of the way you yahoos in this here saloon treated the man, not letting him haunt your joint like he asked. After all, the poor cowboy had no other place to go to.

"And I knew him, or knew *of* him. Feller name of Ben Killpecker owns the Lazy-Bar-K where Butch foremanned. I know ol' Ben from way back. Figured I could do a favor for the deceased cowpoke and my ol' buddy in one swell foop and give you ne'er-do-wells a lick or two while I'm about it.

"Now, ain't you chagrined?" Sam smiled in triumph.

And chagrined I was. The joke was on us.

"But it worked," I pointed out. "Butch's ghost got."

"I told him it'd work and he believed me so it worked. I told you I'd traveled some. T'were no lie. The foolishness folks'll believe and how powerful such belief can be—ain't it amazing?"

"Still, Mick's regained his lost custom," I mused as much to myself as to Sam.

He dismissed this with a backhanded gesture and a puff of cigar smoke. "Look around at who's laughing at who."

I looked around. The bar was crowded and Mick was earning his keep to be sure, but folks pointed and laughed at him and us regulars when they thought we weren't looking, and spoke low so Mick couldn't hear. Banky was getting suspicious that something was amiss as he'd unbuttoned his vest and his gun hand twitched spastic, but he couldn't find anybody to shoot at as the laughers got mighty cautious in their merriment when it came to Banky.

"I dunno," I said, pondering the situation.

"Well, don't let it get in your craw," Sam said. "These folks'll move on after they've had their laugh. This joint won't be open a week from Sunday." He took out a pocket watch, eyed it, grunted, clicked it shut, and repocketed it. "Train leaves in a few minutes, so I'll bid you good day."

He stood to leave. "Oh, one more thing."

"I'm not sure I want to hear—"

"His assailants didn't get Butch's whole poke. He'd stashed a good portion of it before and told me where at. I dug it up and I got it in my bag now. The money is my reward for helping him get revenge on you boys."

With that, Sam Something, newspaper reporter, strode off, laughing.

And I got me an idea of how to salvage something from what might otherwise be the Lucky Nickel's last few days.

RUMOR spread quick around Laramie, and in time throughout

Wyoming and the entire West, that Butch Parker's murderers hadn't got his whole poke. Rumor says he'd stashed a good portion of it before and told us regulars at the Lucky Nickel, in gratitude for our hospitality (for where else would a ghost find such hospitality but right here?) where it was at. Rumor says, if you drop by and buy one or more of the regulars a drink or two, or three, you might get somebody to loosen their tongue enough to tell you where the treasure is stowed. You might could even buy yourself a map. Or two.

Now, ain't that amazing?

THE GRIM REAPER DROPS BY

IT was still forenoon and nobody else in the Lucky Nickel Saloon but us regulars when the Grim Reaper pushed through the batwing doors.

Outside, the August sun beat down relentless on dusty Second Avenue. Inside, it was cool and tranquil, which is how us regulars like it.

"What'll it be, stranger?" Mick the barkeep asked, looking up from his glass-buffing duties at the bar. He cupped his ear to hear better.

"Whiskey," a voice from the bottom of a grave demanded. "Bring the bottle." The batwing doors squeaked shut behind him as he entered, padded softly across the sawdust floor, and took a table.

Mick frowned and focused at the odd-appearing stranger, as did we all—me, Banky with gun-hand aquiver near his ever-ready Colt, and Casper with his one good eye. Charlie lay passed out and Jack Thatcher hadn't arrived yet.

"Lordy be," Mick muttered and crossed himself, a good Irishman. "It's the Banshee."

"Well, what tribe is that, Tom?" Casper inquired of me. His good eye watered from the jalapenos he'd been munching and he couldn't focus worth diddly, which makes it hard to tell the Angel of Death from an Indian.

"Ain't no tribe, Casper," I informed him. "It's trouble for certain sure."

Casper blinked, focused and exclaimed, "Well, I'll be left for dead." He wiped his sweaty forehead with a trembly hand.

"Reckon I ought to persuade him to skedaddle?" Banky offered, as he crouched in his ready-to-shoot stance.

Mick considered, sucking on his teeth and tugging at his prodigious black mustache. "Don't guess you ought, Banky."

"Whyfor not?"

"The feller ain't toting iron, for one."

Gunless. Indeed the feller looked like a Spanish monk, all decked out in a horseshit-brown robe from head to foot. The robe hood was so big a guy couldn't see the face hidden deep within, which was maybe a good thing, as what we could see of his parts like to make your skin crawl right off your body. Which may have been what had happened to our guest. The hands protruding from the huge robe sleeves were naught but skeletal appendages.

Bones, just bones. Skinless, like his feet, sticking out from under the tattered, dusty robe fringe. Yet the hands twitched with such animation as one sees in a guy impatiently waiting for a barkeep to fetch up his drink. As we discovered was the case in this instance.

"I believe I just ordered a whiskey," the voice, like a cold wind at midnight, recalled.

"Besides," Mick went on, "gunplay this early might retard the day's commerce a touch."

I figured gunfire might lure in a few customers, curious ones, who otherwise might not be thirsty, but it was Mick's bar so I didn't say squat.

"I believe I just ordered—"

"Besides, we ain't made the feller's acquaintance yet."

"—a whiskey, bring the bottle." He tossed a half dollar on the table.

"Besides, he paid in advance." Mick brought a glass and a bottle and scooped up the half dollar, which he examined as he returned to the bar.

"Well, 'scuse me." Casper sidling up to the stranger. "You look like, uh, that is, uh—"

"Who's going to get killed?" Banky interjected.

A skeletal hand grabbed the bottle and splashed a shot into the glass. The other bony hand brought the glass into the dismal dark cave of the stranger's hood and the hood tipped back a tad. We heard gulping noises emerge from within. Soon, the glass emerged, empty, slapped on the table with a wet smack and the feller intoned, "I am the Grim Reaper and I have come."

"We got that part figured out, Mister Reaper, sir," I agreed, "but what we ain't got figured is whyfor."

"I am the Grim Reaper and I have come," again came the sepulchral retort, a touch whiny.

Just then, Charlie woke up.

He struggled to the semblance of an upright stance, shaky as a snake with a crutch, and tried to focus on the Reaper.

"Land O' Goshen," Charlie uttered when he saw. Then he eyed the near empty gin bottle he held and raised his arm as if to cast it away. Instead, he shrugged and gulped the gin. "Mick, how about one on the house," he said tearfully, "on account of it's a going-away present?"

Mick didn't have time to ponder his friend's request for Charlie passed out again.

Banky drew lightning quick and aimed his Colt Grim Reaperwards. "Charlie's my friend, you no-good dirty rotten dadgum low-down yellow-bellied son of a snake in the grass—"

The Angel of Death waved a dismissive bony gesture as if to say it wasn't Charlie for whom he'd come. "I am the Grim Reaper and..."

"We got all that part," I repeated. "What we want to know is whyfor have you come."

"Yeah," Banky demanded, squinting down his sights. "Who you come to reap?"

The Grim Reaper held up a bony finger as if to say "Hold your horses," removed a notebook from his robe and flipped it open. "I've come for—"

Just then Jack Thatcher hobbled in through the batwing doors. He stood and wiped his sweaty face with a bandanna and put it back in his pocket. Then he saw. He took one look, eyes bugged out. He pointed with his cane and insisted, "Why you, you—you're..."

"I'm the Grim Reaper and I've—"

Jack Thatcher screamed and lit out, leg, stump, and cane flying every whichaway.

"Now you've gone and done it," Mick growled. "Jack Thatcher's a regular and a friend. Pays his bills, usually, and today's payday and now you've chased him off."

Knobby shoulders shrugged inside the Reaper's robes. He inserted another shot into his hood cave and, I reckon, took a drink. Leastwise the glass emerged empty.

"Well, what ought we to do?" Casper wondered.

"I figure I know what." Banky fired six rounds from his Colt at the ghoulish figure so fast it sounded like Spanish castanets. We expected we'd be engaged in grisly mop duty, but no. The wall behind the Grim Reaper was newly holed and splintered but Banky's target remained unshot.

"Huh," Banky remarked as he blew smoke from the Colt barrel and reloaded. He'd been but four paces away when he let fly. "Do you reckon I stood too close?"

Mick gestured to us for a huddle. We grouped at the bar, beyond the Grim Reaper's earshot—If he had ears.

"What ought we to do?" Mick asked.

"That," I nodded at our visitor, "will spoil folks' thirst for certain sure."

"Reckon you're right," Mick agreed. "We got to do something or I'm bankrupt."

"Well, what?" Casper demanded.

"You don't figure I can earn my daily bread off you regulars, do you?" Mick continued. "I mean, you pay your tabs on time, most often, but it ain't your trade I depend on. I require the occasional passing through cowboy or townie or stranger for my income."

"Why don't we just ask him to leave?" I suggested.

Casper, Banky, and Mick shrugged.

Mick sauntered over to the Grim Reaper's table. "Begging your pardon, Mister Grim Reaper, sir." He cleared his throat. "Me and the boys was wondering, that is, I run a tranquil place here and it might not be as exciting as you're used to. Anyway, uh, we was wondering if you mightn't choose a more raucous saloon in which to wait for your, uh, charge. Or whatever you call 'em when you come for 'em."

"Client," the Grim Reaper intoned. "I provide a service."

"Yes, well, that's nice," Mick agreed. "But we was wondering..."

The Grim Reaper held up a bony finger to interrupt. He removed his notebook again, reminded me of that reporter fellow who drops by occasional, flipped a few pages, and read to himself, I reckon, moving a fingerbone along the page. At last he flipped the book closed and tucked it away. "Nope," he insisted, graveyard-voiced. "This here's the place."

Just then Jack Thatcher hobbled back in with Preacher Avery Morgan in tow.

"Welcome, uh, Brother Morgan." Mick spat on his hand and offered it to shake. Brother Morgan extended his hand. Then he saw the reason for his presence.

"Is that," he pointed, "is that, is that—"

"Reckon so," Banky confirmed.

The preacher took a breath and declared his intentions. "Brother Thatcher brought me forth to exorcise the demon. And even though this ain't exactly the House o' God, I 'spect y'all're decent God-fearing gents, leastwise when you ain't too liquored up. Tenny rate, it don't bode well for decent folk to have such as him in our midst."

We all agreed and Mick offered the preacher a drink to steel him to the disagreeable but necessary task ahead. The preacher nodded gratitude and proceeded to fill up his courage.

It soon became remarkable how much courage it took to fortify him. "Wrestling with Satan's minions is thirsty work," he informed us, "and requires a great deal o' fortification."

He added, "'Sides, it's hot outside."

I could see Mick calculate his on-the-house preacher fortification costs versus the lost trade the preacher's exorcism would restore and how long it'd take before one canceled the other's benefit. His mustache danced on his upper lip like a cat in a hot skillet. Then his eyebrows climbed back up his forehead far enough to merge with his receding hair, he went all goggle-eyed, and exclaimed in horror.

"Well, what?" Casper inquired solicitously.

"Bankruptcy," Mick managed to gasp. "Dire and imminent."

"Exactly what," I posed, "does that mean to us regulars?"

"Closing the Lucky Nickel," Mick gasped. He looked pale.

As did we all.

"Reckon you best get to exorcising," Banky prompted the preacher at gunpoint. I didn't figure Banky would really ventilate him, but you never knew. The situation was dire.

So we had ourselves an exorcism in the Lucky Nickel. And why not? We'd had a wedding, once. The preacher chanted in Latin, I guess, and danced around as if his boots were on fire. He chucked holy water, I guess, Grim Reaperwards, and waved his arms around as if conducting the Mormon Tabernacle Choir or swatting away flies.

Nothing.

The preacher stood afore the Reaper, panting, sweating, defeated. "How come you ain't been vanquished?" he asked.

The Grim Reaper shrugged. Then he crooked a finger at the preacher in a come-here gesture. The preacher looked around at us. He met nary an eye as we all found other places to look—I discovered I needed to clean my fingernails—so he recast his weary glance at the patient, robed skeleton at the table.

Reluctantly, he stepped forward and bent an ear to the cave of the Reaper's hood. We heard the buzz of his graveyard voice whisper to the preacher but strain as we did—Jack Thatcher lost his balance from leaning over and fell down—we couldn't make out a word.

Presently, the preacher stood, gasped like a caught trout and muttered, "Boys, I'm moving to Boise." He marched to the door. "Right now."

Heading out the batwing doors, he bumped into Sam Something, our infrequent semi-regular traveling-through reporter, but not infrequent enough for my taste, just in off the westbound train, dropped by to say hello and see what's what. I saw he had that danged itty-bitty notebook staring out of his vest pocket.

"I heard about the commotion," he declared around his smelly five-cent cigar and that thatchy white mustache. "I got time, so I figured I'd drop by and have a looksee. Hot, ain't it?" He wiped his brow with a kerchief from his hind pocket.

Mick set up Sam with a whiskey and told him about the feller across the room, including the part about how he expected bankruptcy if the Grim Reaper stayed too long.

Sam moseyed over to the table, drink in hand. He bent at the waist and gazed up into the deep pit of the Reaper's hood. He ahemed. "Pardon me, Mister Reaper, good sir. I'm a reporter and I'd like to interview you. Would you be averse—"

"I'll have another bottle of whiskey," the Grim Reaper said to Mick. He tossed a half dollar across the room and Mick caught it with an overhand grab.

Mick shrugged and brought another bottle.

Sam snorted. "I never thought I'd see the day." He walked away from the Reaper and back to the bar. "Everybody wants to be in the paper."

As we discussed our dilemma, a number of folk dropped by. They'd caught wind of our predicament, as had Sam, and had stopped by to see for themselves. A few gawkers tried to see who or what resided inside the deep cowl. None saw.

Mick bravely fought back tears as he explained the Grim Reaper'd drive away customers and he'd be forced to close. Many a toast got lifted in salute to the soon-to-be shut Lucky Nickel and many a sad tear spilled on the sawdust floor.

And, as it was a hot day, yet more people came in, took a gander at the Grim Reaper and ordered a drink and commiserated with Mick's dire straits.

"I got it," Sam hollered, finger upthrust for emphasis.

"Well, what?" Casper prompted.

The crowd fell silent. "I've traveled thither and yon—worldwide, that is, and I've learnt the ways of many a heathen race. The Hindoo of Hindoostan, the pashas of Pakistan, the Turks and bearded shamans of the vast steppes of Asia—"

"What's your point?" Banky urged. We'd all heard this afore, too many times.

Sam eyed the Grim Reaper across the room. The crowd had given the Reaper a wide space around the table at which he sat, alone, nursing his second whiskey bottle.

Sam whispered and those assembled leaned in to hear, except for Mick, who couldn't hear worth diddly anyway, and who stood his ground behind the bar. "Voodoo," is what he said, and commenced to explain a ritual he said he'd learned in the steamy jungles of Siam.

I had reason to be skeptical, but I said naught, as none of us had any plan worth diddly.

In a moment, the rapt listeners who had formed a circle four or five bodies deep around Sam parted to allow the reporter to pass. Sam walked up to the Grim Reaper and the crowd moved across the room, re-forming around the two.

Sam commenced to gibber and holler and dance up and down as if he had a frog in his drawers. The Grim Reaper sat and sipped his drink, I suppose, in silence.

Grim silence.

At last, sweaty and panting, Sam gave up. "Dunno whyfor it don't work." He shrugged and somebody brought him a drink.

It had gotten on to late afternoon, hotter than a two-dollar whore. Sam had become so entranced in the local situation he decided to linger until the next train came through. More folk drifted in off Second Ave to see what's up.

Mick set 'em up as fast as they ordered, sniffling and forcing a smile as he told his customers about his pending unemployment. The sawdust floor got downright soggy with tears.

The Grim Reaper finished his third whiskey bottle as the sun set. It was standing room only in the Lucky Nickel. Somebody had dusted off the old piano in the corner and attempted to play tunes on it, somebody else fell off a table on which they'd been dancing and broke an arm, the entire Ladies' Temperance Union stopped by, singing hymns to celebrate the saloon's pending closure, Charlie woke up, Emma Drummond stopped by, and Jack Thatcher came in.

When Banky decided to do some target practice, shooting cockroaches on the wall, the Grim Reaper stood.

He hadn't stood since he'd sat down that morn and ordered his first bottle. Not even to pee. And when he did stand, the saloon, its walls vibrating with the hoot and holler of four score conversations, got real quiet.

The Grim Reaper looked around at the patrons. The grim patrons looked back. Silence continued.

At last, the Reaper sighed, wind through a fresh grave, and sauntered to the bar, the crowd parting as he passed.

"Barkeep," he announced, "I'll be moving on." He walked to the batwing doors, where he stopped and looked back.

"Whyever for?" Mick wondered, brave smile wavering a tad.

"Well," Casper upped, "ain't you going to, uh, you know—"

"Ain't you going to reap nobody?" Banky finished the question. "Ain't that what you come for?"

"I am the Grim Reaper and I have come," he raised a fingerbone for emphasis, *"for a vacation."*

He sighed and shook his big hood. "Noisy and rowdy I can get any day on the job what with wars and shoot-outs and baseball games and elections and such like. I came here because I heard talk—even in Hell, I heard talk—about how tranquil the Lucky Nickel Saloon, Second Avenue, Laramie, Wyoming, U-S-of-A, is."

He pushed open the batwing doors and turned back again. "Barkeep, your reputation is much overblown. You are not as advertised."

He left.

Presently, the crowd thinned out. Mick lit a few lamps and bid a few customers good night, those sober enough to bid him good night in return. The last unconscious patron got hauled out before dinnertime.

Sam Something went off to find a hotel room, muttering that his voodoo must have worked, but with a delayed reaction.

Soon, nobody remained but us regulars.

"Well," Casper winked at Mick, "I reckon you'll be glad to see that reaper guy," he tilted his head at the door, *"gone."*

Mick buffed glasses behind the bar, frowning.

"Yeah," Banky added. "And nobody got killed today."

Mick sighed, buffed.

"And being shut of him," I concluded, "you won't have to close up."

Mick nodded, buffed. His lower lip trembled.

"I shudder to think," Jack Thatcher shuddered, "of the Lucky Nickel closed on account of him."

Mick sniffled and wiped his nose.

"Imagine," Charlie imagined, "that feller chasing away all your customers. Maybe even us regulars. Imagine—"

Mick bust out crying. Great gobs of tears rolled down his round, red cheeks into his beard and his big shoulders shook with sobs as he buffed the glasses.

The tranquil ambiance for which the Lucky Nickel had come to be known throughout the West and in Hell itself had been restored when the Grim Reaper left. I figured Mick would be happy to have his reputation back unsullied.

But no. Mick's weeping and wailing went on until us regulars tired of it and left to get some peace and quiet. And when we did, Mick just cried even louder.

Darned if I can figure out whyfor.

CHARLIE'S IN THE BOTTLE

POP.

Charlie disappeared.

He'd been sitting at a table toward the back of the Lucky Nickel, his usual table, arguing with Banky. Then Banky said something that sounded Chinese, Greek or maybe Irish and—

Pop.

Charlie disappeared.

We found him quick enough. He was in a gin bottle on the table where he'd been sitting, an empty bottle, luckily, as Charlie couldn't swim. I imagine swimming in gin might be just as irksome as being disappeared, shrunk, and popped into an empty gin bottle. But since these things had never happened to me, I couldn't say for sure how Charlie felt.

He stood in the bottle, cupped hands to his mouth, and shouted something up. Everybody had become quite agitated when Charlie disappeared and even more so when they discovered him in the bottle. They were as noisy as a pugilist crowd, except for Banky who had passed out. I hushed everybody so I could hear. I cleared out some earwax with my little finger, bent to the bottle mouth and listened.

"Say again, Charlie."

"Get me out of here, Tom," he yelled.

Nobody else in the room heard him but me since he was so tiny, a half-inch tall, and thus endowed with tiny lungs. He sounded like a flea might sound if a flea took a notion to talk.

Except for Mick behind the bar, who stood his ground there, the men in the saloon backed away, giving Charlie, the bottle he was in, the table on which the bottle sat, and under which Banky lay unconscious, plenty of room. Maybe they thought if they got too close they'd get sucked into the bottle, too. The same thought had occurred to me but I figured Charlie was no bigger than a ten-day mustache hair because Banky said something magic. And since Banky had passed out, I figured it was safe.

Of course, I kept one wary eye on Banky laying in a sodden

lump under the table. If Banky so much as broke wind, I intended to be in Denver before the smell hit.

Well, if it hadn't been something political that riled Banky enough to shrink his buddy, since Banky was a Democrat and Charlie a Republican, it would have been baseball. Baseball was big in Wyoming at the time. Banky and Charlie enjoyed the occasional friendly argument, politics and baseball being the subjects of choice, mostly.

But nevermind why Banky shrunk his buddy. How the blue blazes, excuse my French, were we going to help poor old Charlie?

Getting him out of the bottle wasn't the problem. He was tiny enough he'd drop right out if we upended the bottle. Getting him unshrunk was the problem.

I relayed Charlie's reasonable request to my colleagues. It was forenoon and the only gents in the room besides Charlie and Banky were me and Casper, plus Mick and that smart-assed reporter Sam Something, back again and between trains. Jack Thatcher hadn't arrived yet.

"Well, it's obvious, ain't it?" Casper intoned. He flipped up his eye patch, took out his glass eye, and buffed it on his sleeve.

"What?" Mick asked, cupping a hand to his ear.

"Well, we got to wake old Banky up and get him to say what he said that got Charlie in this fix, but say it backward so poor Charlie can get out of it." He put his eye back in, lowered the eye patch and blinked vigorously.

"One problem," Sam cautioned.

"What?" Mick observed.

"Fellow's passed out," Sam indicated. He tugged at his mustache and relit his cigar. "Whatever your friend here—"

"Banky," I informed the gentleman. "Short for Bancroft." His discourtesy could be forgiven, as he wasn't a regular.

"—Banky," Sam resumed. "Sorry. I forgot. He said what he said not under the influence of alcohol, I assure you gentlemen. No. Rather, he was under the influence of spirits of another kind. Spirits from beyond the veil."

"What?" Mick required.

"Spiritism?" Casper put in. "Well, haw."

I stayed shut up, as did the unconscious Banky. If Charlie could hear the reporter pontificate from his vantage in the bottle, he didn't say. And if he did, we couldn't hear.

"Spiritism," Sam confirmed, nodding his shaggy mane sagely. "I've seen it on Mississippi riverboats and on wagon trains, seen it from Saint Louie to New Orleans, from the Potomac to the Sacramento. I've seen it from the bayou to the boardwalk, in the mining camps and among the Indians. I've seen it from sea to shining sea—"

"What then," I requested to forestall what seemed to be the first leg of a long, windy story, "do we do?"

"What?" Mick inquired.

"Sobriety," Sam declared, "would be unproductive in this case. No sir. You must induce Mr. Bancroft to consume more gin to reproduce the state he was in when the spirits used him to abuse the unfortunate Mr., uh, Charles—"

"Charlie," I informed Sam, whose pomposity rankled long past endurance, like a burr under a saddle. "Mr. Charles Enright, whom we call 'Charlie.'"

"Indeed," Sam conceded. "Charlie. No offense meant, sir. I forgot. I'm only trying to help."

"Well, let me get this straight," Casper interjected. "We wake Banky up, get him drunk and, what? Let these, uh, spirits, speak through him again?"

"It seems the solution," Sam declared.

"Well, what if these spirits put somebody else in the bottle with Charlie? Maybe me or maybe even you?"

Sam shook his head, frowning. "Consider what Banky said the second before Charlie disappeared *here*—" he pointed to the now-empty chair where Charlie had 'popped' out of thin air "—and reappeared *here*." He gestured toward the bottle in which Charlie had sat down. Charlie looked forlorn.

"Well, I don't recall rightly what he said," Casper admitted.

"What?" Mick inquired.

"Sounded to me something like—" and here Sam made noises that sounded Italian but without the vigorous hand wiggling.

Pop.

Casper disappeared.

We found him in short order, in the bottle.

"Oops," Sam commented.

"What?" Mick offered.

I turned on the reporter with murderous intent but before I could thrash him, it came to me to ask how he knew the exact words Banky, who had begun to awaken, had used to shrink Charlie.

"A good memory for details," Sam muttered, chin bobbing in distress. "It's an asset in my profession. When one can't take notes in the field, memory must suffice. During a battle, for instance, or while astride a horse being pursued by a band of blood-thirsty savages across the plain, or on a tall ship during a blow, I find it—"

"Nevermind all that," I insisted. He could remember what happened during an Indian attack but couldn't remember our names? "What're we going to do to get him back?"

"What?" Mick queried.

Sam looked quite sorrowful. "I'm truly sorry. I had no idea that repeating—"

"Nevermind all that." The fellow was much too windy for my taste. "Can you undo it?"

At that point, Charlie swayed through the front batwing doors, collar askew, suspenders hanging, hair tangled, looking disheveled but quite the old Charlie we knew before he got shrunk.

A closer look at the bottle on the table revealed Casper inside jumping up and down and shouting his flea-sized lungs out, but no Charlie in the bottle. No, Charlie stood amid his back-thumping, relieved, welcoming cronies, which now included Banky, who had emerged from his slumber to stand pasty-faced and as wobble-legged as a newborn colt.

Sam looked somber, as if he'd et something disagreeable or Mexican. As for me, I was relieved right enough to see Charlie out of his fix, but distressed that Casper was now in the same fix and I had a few questions for both Banky and Sam. I suspected Sam hadn't been candid with us, no surprise.

"I believe, sir," I confronted Sam, "you have some explaining to do."

My tone suggested seriousness and the others in the room—Mick, Banky, and Charlie—quit their fussing and paid attention.

"What?" Mick prompted.

Sam ahemed and shuffled feet. "Well, I didn't exactly say exactly what Banky said when he said what he said that put Charlie in the bottle—"

"But what you said put Casper in the bottle," I pointed out.

"And got me out, I reckon, at the same time," Charlie contributed.

"Yes," Sam conceded, "the phenomena appear linked."

"And something else," Charlie offered. "When Banky said what he said and I ended up in that bottle, I had me the worst cold I've had since my days in Saskatoon, I swear. But I don't now."

"You figure I cured you or something?" Banky inquired, voice slurry, like he was talking Swedish or gargling or suchlike.

This prompted vigorous verbiage among all present, except for

Casper who we couldn't hear and Mick who just said "What?" During this exchange, Sam allowed as how the incantation Banky incanted, and which he'd confessedly botched, sounded Hindoo to him. Banky admitted he'd seen a VooDoo Negress that a.m. to treat a painful ingrown toenail and left a dispute over the fee unresolved. As a result, although she had cured his ailment, the woman may have also cursed him.

Whereupon Charlie reminded us, it may not have been a curse.

"What?" Mick wondered.

"I had this cold afore," Charlie recalled. "Now I don't. I think getting shrunk and all made my cold go away."

"But when you got unshrunk," Sam noted, "Casper was. Shrunk, that is."

We stood in silence for a moment taking in the implications. Casper could be heard stomping around inside his bottle like a fly against a window.

"One way to figure it out," Sam decided.

"What?" Mick asked.

"Repeat the experiment."

"But how?" I wondered. "You confessed that what you said that shrunk Casper and deshrunk Charlie wasn't exactly what Banky said in the first place to shrink Charlie—"

"For which I'm mighty sorry, old friend," Banky apologized, a sob in his throat.

"Banky, my good man," Sam patted Banky's shoulder in an annoying, paternal gesture, "can you remember what you said to Charlie when he, uh, you know—"

"Not a blamed word," Banky uttered. "I was drunk at the time."

"Charlie, can you remember—"

"Not word for word, I reckon," Charlie shook his head. "But close enough to try. And if it'll save our friend Casper there in the bottle, I'm willing to give it a try."

I suspect Casper heard this last, as his head commenced to frantic bobbing up and down and I could hear his squeaking agreement in a fairy voice.

I bent my ear to the bottle. "I figure you got to be looking at whoever gets popped," Casper called out to me.

I gave him the okay sign and told the others. They already had that part figured.

We all gathered around Charlie, except for Casper. The swaying Banky, the bewildered-seeming Mick, Sam with stogie ablaze, and me, we all stood shoulder to shoulder in solidarity with Charlie as he tried to recall what Banky had said.

All I got was mumble, mumble, you low-down no-good yakity-yakity, yellow-bellied, son-of-a so on and so forth, blah, blah, blah. And such like. I had the impression Charlie was making up what he said he remembered Banky say, and it didn't resemble at all what Sam had said he'd remembered Banky saying when Sam had said what he said Banky said.

Pop.

Mick disappeared.

And Casper fell down from midair and broke a table and Mick was in the bottle and Casper tried to stand and shake off the spittoon in which he'd lodged a boot when he fell.

"Well, it works," Casper declared. He shook the spittoon off with a jerk, flipped his eye patch up on his forehead, and blinked.

If Mick said "What?" nobody heard.

"Well, I can see," Casper cried out in joy.

And he could. Since that time his rifle backfired poking his eye out, Casper hadn't seen anything three-dimensional. Now he saw as clear-eyed as Annie Oakley.

Backslapping and raucous yipping commenced to celebrate Casper's good fortune.

Which abated as the assembled realized with chagrin that Mick was now in the fix Casper had been in and Charlie had been in before Casper.

"If Mick is to resume his rightful place behind the bar," I submitted, "one of us will have to say some magic words—"

"And it doesn't seem critical who says it or what they say, exactly," Sam interjected. "At least for it to work."

"—and put another of us in Mick's place."

I don't recall who noted I hadn't had a turn in the bottle yet.

Not me, no sir. I felt no need to see the world from the bottom of a gin bottle, thank you, and I felt as healthy as a muleskinner and in no need of medication, magical or otherwise.

I was saved the awkwardness of objecting aloud to aiding Mick out of the bottle by the timely arrival of Jack Thatcher, who hobbled to his usual seat.

We all stared at Jack, thinking up a storm.

"Say," Jack called out, tapping his cane against the table as if to wake us up, "what are you all doing that's so important you forget to say hello to your friends and to stare so?"

We continued to stare at Jack as if he had spoken Chinese. Then we stared at each other, and at Mick, who'd gone quiet in the bottle.

"Well, how's the leg?" Casper finally enquired.

Jack shrugged. "Could be better."

We brought Jack up to date, and Casper showed off his two good eyes. We decided I would say what I recalled the others having said and pop Jack into the bottle, so as to restore Mick and fix up Jack to boot.

While we were talking so, Sam dismissed himself and sauntered out back to the privy to pee.

That's when we boys added a little twist to our plans.

So Sam rejoined us and I said my say and Jack appeared in the bottle and Mick came walking through the back door from the alley where he had reappeared. And, yes, Mick could hear quite well. Rather than say "What?" all the time, he took to saying "Pipe down" a lot.

Inside the gin bottle, Jack tossed aside his cane and danced a jig on both legs, restored. He "yipped," as did we all.

"Now, Sam," I said rubbing my hands together, "I've noticed that you, uh, that is—"

"You pee a lot," Banky said. "And didn't you say once that it burns?"

Sam nodded, admitting his affliction.

It took some doing, but he got persuaded.

Mick did the honors.

Pop.

MOSTLY, the Lucky Nickel Saloon, Second Avenue, Laramie, Wyoming, U-S of A, is a quiet, tranquil place, which is how us regulars like it. Now and then, you'll hear stories about the goings on in our little dive that would make you speculate that once or twice it got a little exciting here.

There's one story about a dragon nobody ever saw, and about this mermaid who got married here, and about this fellow who got killed out back and then came in for a drink, and even a story about the day the Angel of Death stopped by.

There's a story about some magical bottle.

Nobody ever saw that dragon. The mermaid and her husband never came back. That ghost vanished. Ditto the Grim Reaper.

There ain't nothing here to prove any of these things ever really happened. They're just stories.

Except.

"Say, barkeep?"

"Hm?"

"What's that?" Pointing at a gin bottle on a polished walnut shelf behind the bar.

"A gin bottle."

"Yeah, but what's that in it?"

"Nobody."

"Nobody?"

"I mean—nothing."

END

ABOUT THE AUTHOR

Ex-reporter and former Wyominger Ken Rand resides in Utah where he writes   semi-fulltime.

He's sold fiction to Weird Tales, Aboriginal SF, On Spec, Writers of the Future, Star Trek: Strange New Worlds, and four dozen other magazines and anthologies. He wrote The Eternity Stone (The Fiction Works), Phoenix (Zumaya), Voices of Wonder: 20 Interviews in Fantasy and Science Fiction (Wildside Press), and The 10% Solution: Self-editing for the Modern Writer (Fairwood Press).

His website: www.sfwa.org/members/Rand/.

His writing and living philosophy: "Lighten up."

ABOUT THE COVER ARTIST

Keith Berdak has done cover work for many novels including Glen Cook's *Black Company* Series and *Bubbas Of the Apocalypse*, in which his Darrel Award winning short story, "The Fighting 77th," appeared.

Yard Dog Press Titles As Of This Print Date

A Bubba in Time Saves None, Edited by Selina Rosen
A Man, A Plan, (yet lacking) A Canal, Panama, Linda Donahue
Adventures of the Irish Ninja, Selina Rosen
The Alamo and Zombies, Jean Stuntz
All the Marbles, Dusty Rainbolt
Almost Human, Gary Moreau
Ancient Enemy, Lee Killouth
The Anthology From Hell: Humorous Tales From WAY Down Under,
    Edited by Julia S. Mandala
Ard Magister, Laura J. Underwood
Assassins Inc., Phillip Drayer Duncan
Assassins Incorporated: Rehired, Phillip Drayer Duncan
Bad City, Selina Rosen & Laura J. Underwood
Bad Lands, Selina Rosen & Laura J. Underwood
Black Rage, Selina Rosen
Blackrose Avenue, Mark Shepherd
The Boat Man, Selina Rosen
Bobby's Troll, John Lance
Bride of Tranquility, Tracy S. Morris
Bruce and Roxanne from Start to Finnish, Rie Sheridan Rose
The Bubba Chronicles, Selina Rosen
Bubba Fables, Sue P. Sinor
Bubbas Of the Apocalypse, Edited by Selina Rosen
The Burden of the Crown, Selina Rosen
Chains of Redemption, Selina Rosen
Checking On Culture, Lee Killough
Chronicles of the Last War, Laura J. Underwood
Dadgum Martians Invade the Lucky Nickel Saloon, Ken Rand
Dark and Stormy Nights, Bradley H. Sinor
Deja Doo, Edited by Selina Rosen
Dracula's Lawyer, Julia S. Mandala
Dragon's Tongue, Laura J. Underwood
The Essence of Stone, Beverly A. Hale
Fairy BrewHaHa at the Lucky Nickel Saloon, Ken Rand
The Fantastikon: Tales of Wonder, Robin Wayne Bailey
Fire & Ice, Selina Rosen
Flush Fiction, Volume I: Stories To Be Read In One Sitting, Edited by
    Selina Rosen
Flush Fiction, Volume II: Twenty Years of Letting it Go!, Edited by
    Selina Rosen
The Four Bubbas of the Apocalypse: Flatulence, Halitosis, Incest,
    and... Ned, Edited by Selina Rosen
The Four Redheads: Apocalypse Now!, Linda L. Donahue, Rhonda
    Eudaly, Julia S. Mandala, & Dusty Rainbolt
The Four Redheads of the Apocalypse, Linda L. Donahue, Rhonda
    Eudaly, Julia S. Mandala, & Dusty Rainbolt

The Four Redheads: The Wrath of Satan, Linda L. Donahue,
  Rhonda Eudaly, Julia S. Mandala, & Dusty Rainbolt
The Garden In Bloom, Jeffrey Turner
The Geometries of Love: Poetry by Robin Wayne Bailey
The Golems Of Laramie County, Ken Rand
The Green Women, Laura J. Underwood
The Guardians, Lynn Abbey
Hammer Town, Selina Rosen
The Happiness Box, Beverly A. Hale
The Host Series: The Host, Fright Eater, Gang Approval, Selina Rosen
Houston, We've Got Bubbas!, Edited by Selina Rosen
How I Spent the Apocolypse, Selina Rosen
I Didn't Quite Make It To Oz, Edited by Selina Rosen
I Should Have Stayed In Oz, Edited by Selina Rosen
In the Shadows, Bradley H. Sinor
International House of Bubbas, Edited by Selina Rosen
It's the Great Bumpkin, Cletus Brown!, Katherine A. Turski
Judas Gene, Gary Moreau
The Killswitch Review, Steven-Elliot Altman & Diane DeKelb-
  Rittenhouse
The Leopard's Daughter, Lee Killough
The Lightning Horse, John Moore
The Logic of Departure, Mark W. Tiedemann
The Long, Cold Walk To Mars, Jeffrey Turner
Marking the Signs and Other Tales Of Mischief, Laura J. Underwood
Material Things, Selina Rosen
Medieval Misfits: Renaissance Rejects, Tracy S. Morris
Mirror Images, Susan Satterfield
Mirror, Mirror and Other Reflections, James K. Burk
More Stories That Won't Make Your Parents Hurl, Edited by Selina
  Rosen
Music for Four Hands, Louis Antonelli & Edward Morris
My Life with Geeks and Freaks, Claudia Christian
The Necronomicrap: A Guide To Your Horooscope, Tim Frayser
*Of Two Minds: Location Shoot, It's a Miracle, and Other Strange
  Stories*, Bradley H & Sue P. Sinor
The Pinnacle, Gary Moreau
Redheads In Love, Linda L. Donahue, Rhonda Eudaly, Julia S.
  Mandala, & Dusty Rainbolt
Reruns, Selina Rosen
Rock 'n' Roll Universe, Ken Rand
Shadows In Green, Richard Dansky
Stories That Won't Make Your Parents Hurl, Edited by Selina Rosen
Tales from Keltora, Laura J. Underwood
*Tales Of the Lucky Nickel Saloon, Second Ave., Laramie, Wyoming, U S
  of A*, Ken Rand

Tarbox Station, Rhonda Eudaly
Texistani: Indo-Pak Food From A Texas Kitchen, Beverly A. Hale
That's All Folks, J. F. Gonzalez
Through Wyoming Eyes, Ken Rand
Turn Left to Tomorrow, Robin Wayne Bailey
The Twins, Selina Rosen
The Undead Ate My Head, Ethan Nahté
Wandering Lark, Laura J. Underwood
Weirdough, Inc., Selina Rosen & Sherri Dean
Wings of Morning, Katharine Eliska Kimbriel
Zombies In Oz and Other Undead Musings, Robin Wayne Bailey

Double Dog

(A YDP Imprint):

#1:

Of Stars & Shadows,
Mark W. Tiedemann

This Instance Of Me,
Jeffrey Turner

#2:

Gods and Other Children,
Bill D. Allen

Tranquility, Tracy Morris

#3:

Home Is the Hunter,
James K. Burk

Farstep Station,
Lazette Gifford

#4:

Sabre Dance,
Melanie Fletcher

The Lunari Mask,
Laura J. Underwood

#5:

House of Doors,
Julia Mandala

Jaguar Moon,
Linda A. Donahue

Just Cause
(A YDP Imprint):

The Bitter End
Selina Rosen

Death Under the Crescent Moon
Dusty Rainbolt

Duckrt Escapes from Jail
Zeb Rosenzweig

Duckrt: Mystery at the Museum
Zeb Rosenzweig

Getting It Real
Selina Rosen

The Ghost Writer
Selina Rosen

It's Not Rocket Science: Spirituality for the Working-Class Soul
Selina Rosen

Meditations of a Hoarder
Melinda LaFevers

Not My Life
Selina Rosen

The Pit
Selina Rosen

Plots and Protagonists: A Reference Guide for Writers
Mel. White

Vanishing Fame
Selina Rosen

**Fantasy Writers Asylum
(A YDP Imprint):**
Blood Songs
Julia Mandala

Gateway to Corimar
Julia Mandala & Linda L Donahue

Tale of the Black Heart
Linda L. Donahue

Non-YDP titles we distribute:
Chains of Freedom
Chains of Destruction
Jabone's Sword
Queen of Denial
Recycled
Strange Robby
Sword Masters
Selina Rosen

Three Ways to Order:

1. Write us a letter telling us what you want, then send it along with your check or money order (made payable to Yard Dog Press) to: Yard Dog Press, 710 W. Redbud Lane, Alma, AR 72921-7247

2. Use selinarosen@cox.net or lynnstran@cox.net to contact us and place your order. Then send your check or money order to the address above. *This has the advantage of allowing you to check on the availability of short-stock items such as T-shirts and back-issues of Yard Dog Comics.*

3. Contact us as in #1 or #2 above and pay with a credit card or by debit from your checking account. Either give us the credit card information in your letter/Email/phone call, or go to our website and use our shopping carts. If you send us your information, please include your name as it appears on the card, your credit card number, the expiration date, and the 3 or 4-digit security code after your signature on the back (CVV). Please remember that we will include media rate (minimum $3.00) S/H for mailing in the lower 48 states.

*Watch our website at
www.yarddogpress.com
for news of upcoming projects
and new titles!!*

A Note to Our Readers

We at Yard Dog Press understand that many people buy used books because they simply can't afford new ones. That said, and understanding that not everyone is made of money, we'd like you to know something that you may not have realized. Writers only make money on new books that sell. At the big houses a writer's entire future can hinge on the number of books they sell. While this isn't the case at Yard Dog Press, the honest truth is that when you sell or trade your book or let many people read it, the writer and the publishing house aren't making any money.

As much as we'd all like to believe that we can exist on love and sweet potato pie, the truth is we all need money to buy the things essential to our daily lives. Writers and publishers are no different.

We realize that these "freebies" and cheap books often turn people on to new writers and books that they wouldn't otherwise read. However we hope that you will reconsider selling your copy, and that if you trade it or let your friends borrow it, you also pass on the information that if they really like the author's work they should consider buying one of their books at full price sometime so that the writer can afford to continue to write work that entertains you.

We appreciate all our readers and *depend* upon their support.

Thanks,
The Editorial Staff
Yard Dog Press

PS – Please note that "used" books without covers have, in most cases, been stolen. Neither the author nor the publisher has made any money on these books because they were supposed to be pulped for lack of sales.
Please do not purchase books without covers.

www.ingramcontent.com/pod-product-compliance
Lightning Source LLC
Chambersburg PA
CBHW030517130626
46549CB00007B/3037